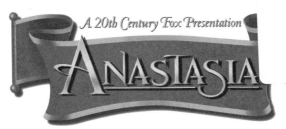

A 20th Century Fox Presentation

ANASTASIA

A Don Bluth / Gary Goldman Film

How to Behave Like a Princess

By Ali Hokin
Illustrated by the Thompson Brothers

 A GOLDEN BOOK • NEW YORK

Golden Books Publishing Company, Inc., New York, New York 10106

Library of Congress Catalog Card Number: 97-71075   ISBN: 0-307-12972-1   A MCMXCVII

$\mathcal{W}$hen word got around that Empress Marie was looking for her long-lost granddaughter, Princess Anastasia, two con artists, Vladimir and Dimitri, decided to audition young girls for the part. They coached the "winners" in the very fine art of how to behave in a proper manner— that is, like a princess. . . .

You don't have to be a princess to behave like one . . .
although it certainly helps if you were born in a palace
by the sea.

A princess never plays with the same toy twice. Instead, she has new ones delivered to her every day.

A princess must sit up straight and stand up tall. She never slouches or slumps. Her hair is always brushed, and her clothes are forever pressed and spotless. Not even a strong breeze will upset a true princess's appearance.

A princess never gulps down her beef Stroganoff. She takes small bites and eats slowly. She never talks with her mouth full, and she always finishes what's on her plate.

A princess always greets others by curtsying and
extending her gloved hand to receive a kiss.

No matter what activity she's engaged in, a princess prefers
to wear long flowing gowns and a golden tiara.

Whether celebrating her birthday or another lost tooth, a princess must always party lavishly.

A princess is so graceful that when she dances the waltz, her feet never seem to touch the ground.

From the bows in her hair to the shoes on her feet, the clothes a princess wears must never be seen twice. In fact, it is her royal duty to change her outfit before each meal and after every activity.

A princess always knows everyone's names, even if she has never met them before. She can recite her family tree as well as her cat's and dog's going back at least two hundred years. She never forgets to mention great-great-great-aunts and distant cousins.

But the fact is, a true princess can break all these rules,
for the simple reason that she is . . . a princess!